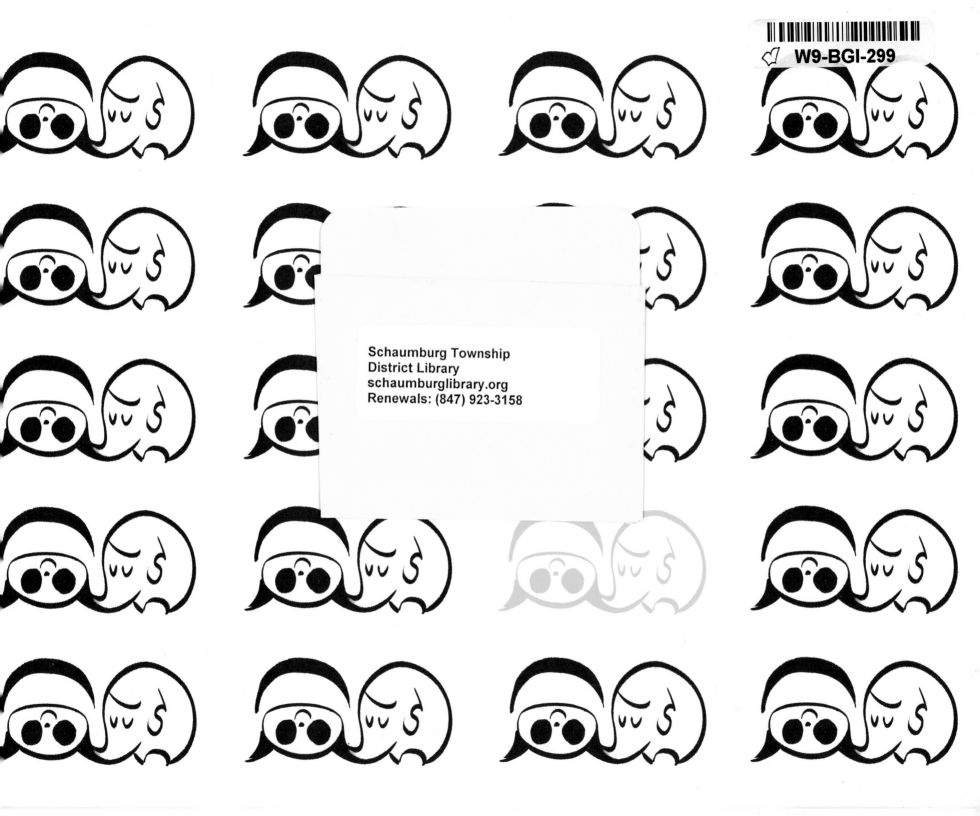

For Penelope and Felicity, who inspire me every day to follow my dreams

First Edition, April 2020
10 9 8 7 6 5 4 3 2 1
FAC- 029191-20052
Printed in Malaysia

This book is set in Otari/TK Type
Designed by Joann Hill and David Hastings
Illustrations created with watercolor, gouache, pencil, and digital media.
Calligraphy on pp. 12–13 and 36 by Mau Keung Wu.
Other calligraphy by Raymond Tam and Maria Lee.
Library of Congress Control Number: 2019943658

ISBN 978-1-368-01000-9
Reinforced binding
Visit www.DisneyBooks.com

Ellie

Makes a Friend

by Mike Wu

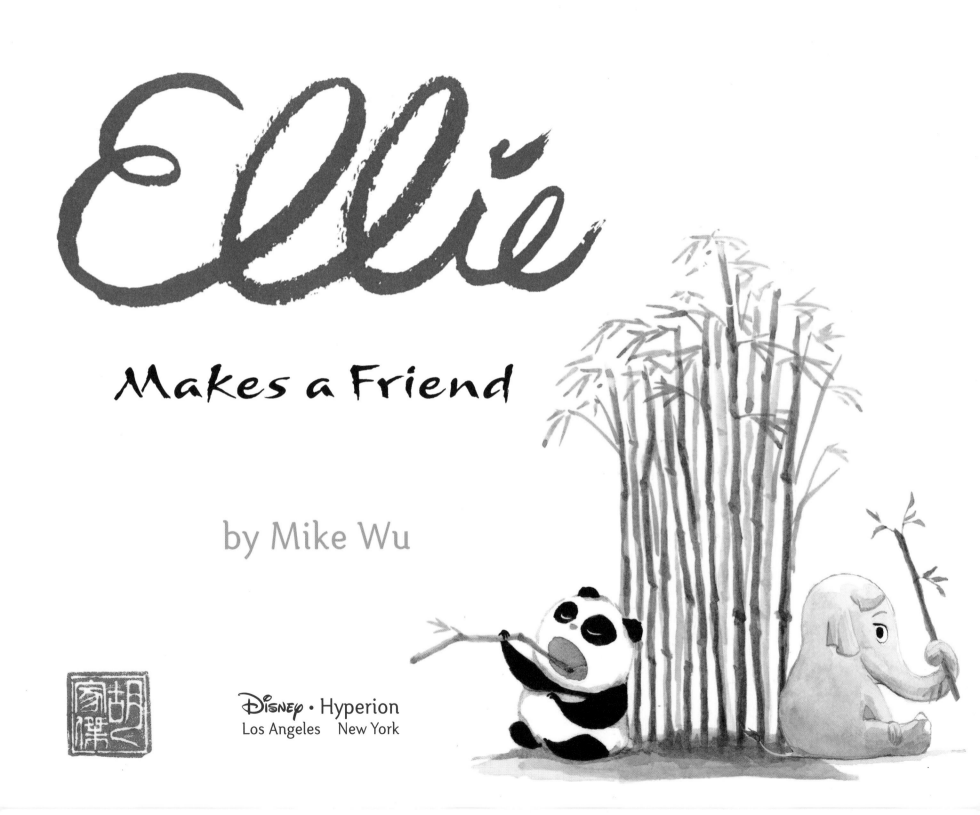

Disney • Hyperion
Los Angeles   New York

CHIRP, BUZZ, GROWL!

On a quiet spring morning, Ellie was just waking up when she heard a cheerful commotion just beyond her walls.

Ellie went to investigate and arrived as Walt began his announcement.

"We have a new friend joining us. Her name is Ping, and she's from a faraway place called China," declared Walt.

Ellie found Lucy and Gerard, and introduced herself to the newcomer. "Hi, my name is Ellie."

Ellie and her friends couldn't understand Ping.
So Ping picked up her brush and painted her words—
but her words looked like pictures.

"Look, Ellie. She's an artist just like you!" exclaimed Lucy.

All the animals marveled at Ping's beautiful brushwork and calligraphy.

Ping offered her bamboo brush to Ellie.
"I already have a brush, thank you," she replied.

Soon Ping was the talk of the zoo.

Even Lucy and Gerard were fans.
"Ping is quite clever," declared Gerard.

"Ping is so talented," said Lucy.

Ping's calligraphy wasn't her only talent.
She would often draw animals, too.

"Maybe my paintings aren't that special," Ellie whispered to herself.

"You and Ping are each special in your own way," Gerard assured her. "You are more alike than you think."

Ellie wanted to know more about Ping and her art.
With Lucy's help, she found there is balance and harmony
in painting with black and white.

Gerard showed Ellie where China is, but Ellie wanted more answers.

So she went to find Ping.

Along the way, Ellie noticed some of Ping's calligraphy on her own paintings.

And when she found Ping, Ellie watched as she drew.
They were starting to understand each other.

As they spent more time together, Ping shared her favorite food,

and how she liked to relax.

This time, when Ping offered her brush . . .

... Ellie gave it a try!

It made her paintings pop in a new and unique way.

With Ellie's brush, Ping added some greens and reds to the painting.

It looked even more vibrant.

The next day, they found a blank space to fill. Ellie painted a color, and Ping made a mark. They continued until their painting danced with balance and harmony.

All the animals gathered to witness the beautiful new art the two had created together, along with Ping's calligraphy.

Ellie read it aloud.

"A friendship begins with sharing."

Before long, the two friends were sharing stories and ideas and creating more amazing art together every day.

Love

Chinese Words

你好 Hello

花 Flower

平 Ping

鳥 Bird

朋友 Friend

愛 Love